W9-COT-203

Wanda and the Wild Hair

Barbara Azore • Illustrated by Georgia Graham

Tundra Books

Published in Canada by Tundra Books,
481 University Avenue, Toronto, Ontario M5G 2E9

Published in the United States by Tundra Books of Northern New York,
P.O. Box 1030, Plattsburgh, New York 12901

Library of Congress Control Number: 2004110121

Library and Archives Canada Cataloguing in Publication

Azore, Barbara
  Wanda and the wild hair / Barbara Azore ; illustrated by Georgia
Graham.

ISBN 0-88776-717-6

I. Graham, Georgia, 1959- II. Title.

PS8601.Z67W35 2005   jC813'.6   C2004-904102-9

We acknowledge the financial support of the Government of Canada
through the Book Publishing Industry Development Program (BPIDP)
and that of the Government of Ontario through the Ontario Media
Development Corporation's Ontario Book Initiative.

We further acknowledge the support of the Canada Council for the Arts
and the Ontario Arts Council for our publishing program.

ONTARIO ARTS COUNCIL
CONSEIL DES ARTS DE L'ONTARIO

Medium: chalk pastel on paper

Design: Terri Nimmo

Printed in Hong Kong, China

1 2 3 4 5 6   10 09 08 07 06 05

For Adrianne, Alex, Jenna, Kara, Lee, and Lois
B.A.

For the Alberta teachers and librarians
who love to read to children
G.G.

Wanda's hair was wild. Really wild. And she loved it. She loved the way it felt when she touched it. Soft and springy like newly cut grass.

She loved the way her bangs shaded her eyes in summer and caught snowflakes in winter.

She hated it when her mother said, "It's time to wash your hair, Wanda."

She loathed it when her father said, "You look like an Old English sheepdog. Why don't you go to the poodle parlor for a trim and brushup?"

She was miserable when her teacher said her hair was like a bush, and made her write fifty times on the blackboard, "I must comb my hair."

When her mother suggested a visit to the hairdresser (which she did every other day), Wanda stamped her foot and said, "No!"

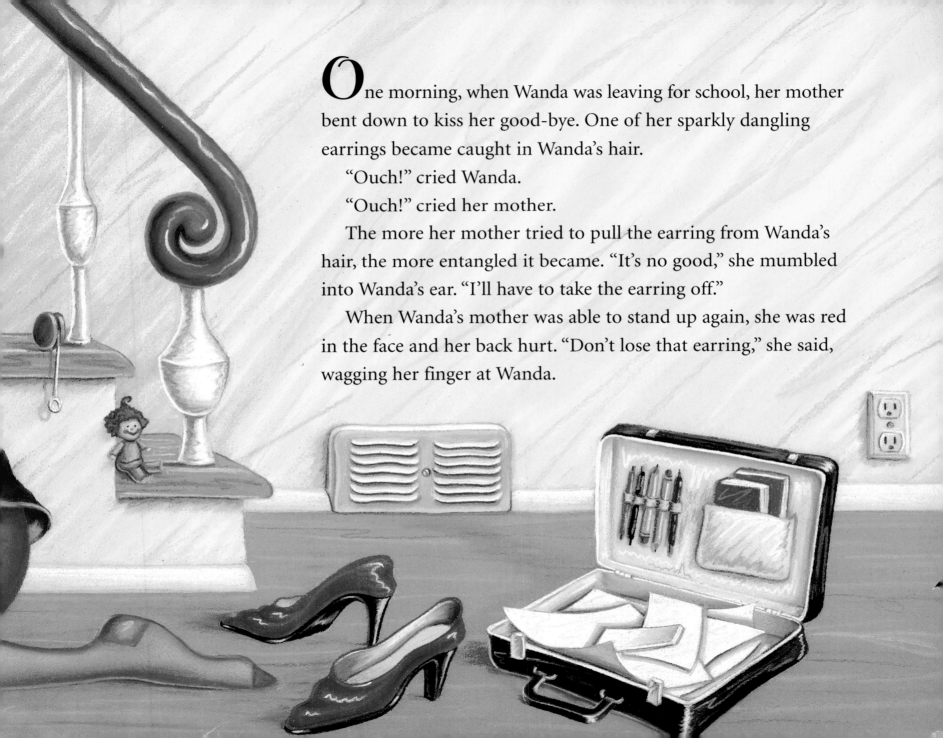

One morning, when Wanda was leaving for school, her mother bent down to kiss her good-bye. One of her sparkly dangling earrings became caught in Wanda's hair.

"Ouch!" cried Wanda.

"Ouch!" cried her mother.

The more her mother tried to pull the earring from Wanda's hair, the more entangled it became. "It's no good," she mumbled into Wanda's ear. "I'll have to take the earring off."

When Wanda's mother was able to stand up again, she was red in the face and her back hurt. "Don't lose that earring," she said, wagging her finger at Wanda.

"I won't!" Wanda called, as she ran down the street. She passed a little old lady taking her large Old English sheepdog for a walk. The dog wagged his tail, and Wanda saw two shiny black eyes peering up at her through long shaggy bangs. "Nice doggy," said Wanda.

At the corner, Mrs. Brown's cat was sitting on the fence watching, through slit eyes, a magpie strutting about on the sidewalk. The magpie flew into a tree as Wanda ran past.

"You need to grow wings," Wanda called to the cat. The cat hissed at her.

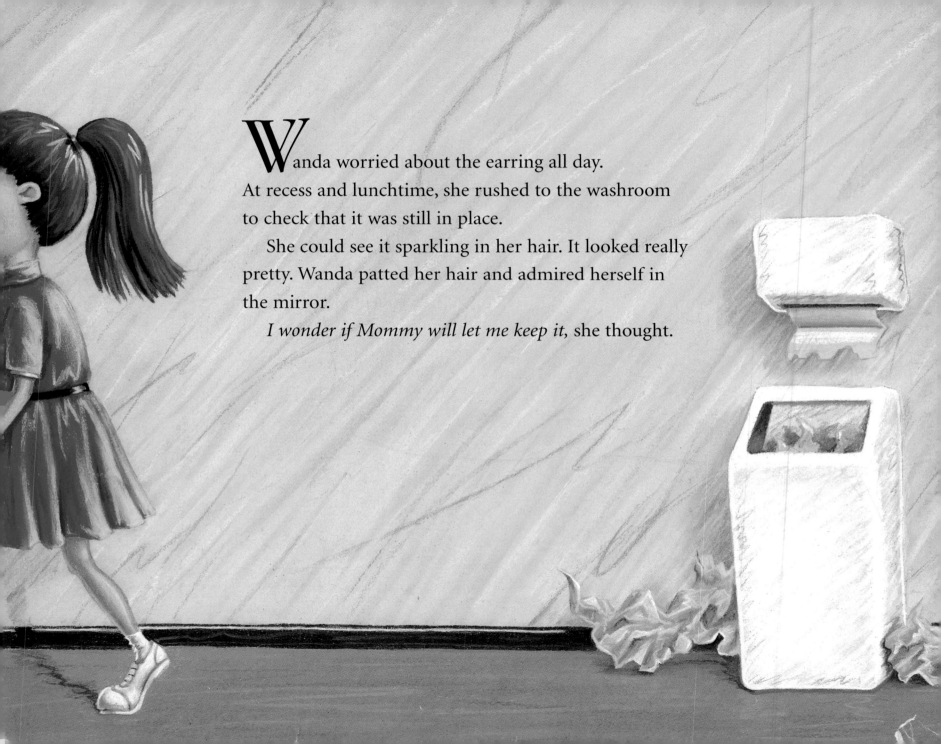

anda worried about the earring all day.
At recess and lunchtime, she rushed to the washroom
to check that it was still in place.

She could see it sparkling in her hair. It looked really
pretty. Wanda patted her hair and admired herself in
the mirror.

I wonder if Mommy will let me keep it, she thought.

Wanda's worry about the earring caused problems all day.

On the softball pitch, she dropped an easy catch. She got paint in her hair using finger paints in art.

During show-and-tell, she checked the earring so many times that her teacher shouted at her: "If you fiddle with your hair one more time, I shall send you to the office and ask the principal to cut it off!"

Wanda was relieved when the bell rang to end school for the day. Once she got home, the earring would be safe.

The sidewalk was covered with fallen leaves. Wanda kicked a crunchy pile as she walked beneath the elm tree. A magpie sitting in the branches above spied the earring shining in Wanda's hair. With a loud caw, he flew down onto Wanda's head and pecked at the earring.

Wanda screamed and began to run, slapping her head to dislodge the bird. At the corner, Mrs. Brown's cat was dozing on the fence post. Startled awake, he saw the magpie and leapt to catch it.

Wanda screeched as the cat landed on her head. The magpie screeched as it flew out of the cat's claws. The cat screeched as the magpie escaped.

Before Wanda could wonder what might happen next, she found herself lying in a pile of dead leaves, with the large Old English sheepdog sitting on her chest. The cat had fled, and the dog was licking her face with a big wet tongue.

Wanda heard running footsteps and someone calling, "Buddy, get off her!"

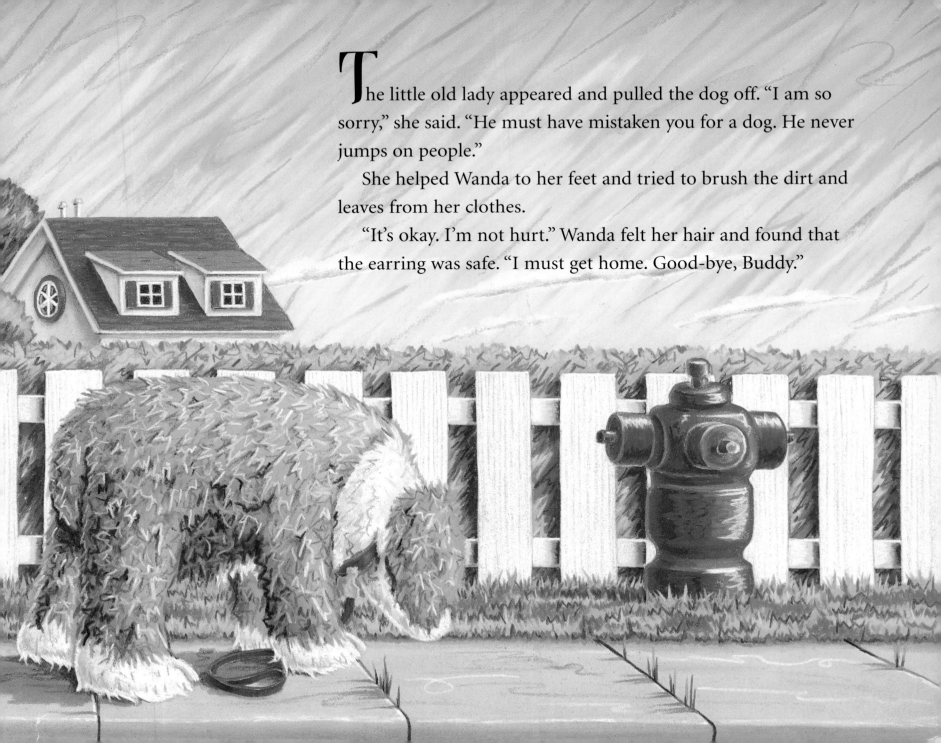

The little old lady appeared and pulled the dog off. "I am so sorry," she said. "He must have mistaken you for a dog. He never jumps on people."

She helped Wanda to her feet and tried to brush the dirt and leaves from her clothes.

"It's okay. I'm not hurt." Wanda felt her hair and found that the earring was safe. "I must get home. Good-bye, Buddy."

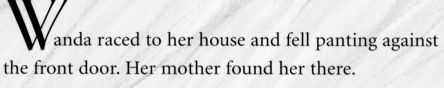anda raced to her house and fell panting against the front door. Her mother found her there.

"What happened to you?" she cried.

Wanda fell into her mother's arms.

"Oh, Mom. A bird tried to steal your earring. Then a cat tried to catch the bird and a great big dog knocked me down. But your earring is still here – somewhere. I think."

"There, there. Never mind about the earring," said her mother. She picked at some of the leaves and twigs, and pulled out a bird feather and a half-eaten dog biscuit covered in cat hair. "You really do look as though you have a bush on your head," she said.

Wanda looked at herself in the mirror. Her mother was right. Her hair *was* matted. Berries, leaves, twigs, an apple, and a magpie feather were poking out in the oddest places. She touched her hair. It felt more like straw than newly cut grass.

"I do think it's time to visit the hairdresser," her mother suggested.

Wanda sighed. "Okay. But just this once."

Humming happily, her mother went to fetch her purse.

The hairdresser, who liked a challenge, attacked Wanda's hair with grim determination. She washed and snipped and dried and brushed, and, when she was finished, stepped back with a satisfied sigh.

Wanda looked in the mirror and smiled. "Don't worry," she whispered to her reflection. "It will soon grow again."